His Alpha Wolf: Gay First Time Romance

Van Cole

Published by Van Cole, 2022.

This is a work of fiction. Similarities to real people, places, or events are entirely coincidental.

HIS ALPHA WOLF: GAY FIRST TIME ROMANCE

First edition. November 25, 2022.

Copyright © 2022 Van Cole.

ISBN: 979-8223972785

Written by Van Cole.

Table of Contents

His Alpha Wolf
Gay First Time Romance

By: Van Cole

Foreword

This wolf runs alone.

Clayton is a werewolf with the blood of an alpha coursing through his veins. After his father's death, it was his duty to take the position of pack leader.

Only, that never happened.

After getting caught up with the wrong man, he succeeded in getting his heart broken and his whole world turned upside down. Before he knew it, he was running alone – a lone wolf.

So, he searched far and wide for his mate.

The one person who could fill the void in his heart.

And he searched for a long, long time.

Until he arrived in a small town. He never expected to stay. But, then again, he never expected to fall in love.

And yet, that's exactly what he did.

He took the chance. He made himself vulnerable.

Will it turn out for the best or will this new lover betray him like the last?

His Alpha Wolf

Chapter 1

The leaves shivered with the wind as the sun slowly crept toward the horizon, painting the faraway landscape in vibrant oranges and a haze of yellow.

A lone figure stepped forward, emerging from the tree line. He rolled his shoulders, nostrils flaring. An array of different smells wafted toward his sensitive nose from the bakery two blocks down to the pancakes cooking in a nearby house, eagerly awaited by two children, giggling among themselves.

For a moment, Clayton Hines remembered his own childhood. It was much different than what "normal" kids experienced. Instead of going to elementary school and learning his ABCs, he learned the art of hunting, of creeping up on his prey, charging forward, and making the kill. His mother was once the fastest of the pack, weaving in and out of the trees, outrunning anything that tried to escape her. His father was a bulk of muscles that rippled underneath his black coat of fur. For a long, long time, his father reigned as the alpha of the pack. He was kind, compassionate, and treated everyone with respect from the lowest omega to the proudest beta.

When the time came, Clayton took his rightful place as alpha, following in his father's footsteps. The pack loved him. Many of the girls tried to mate with him. Even his mother pressured him into finding a partner.

Only, Clayton could not find a female to satisfy him because they didn't attract him the way men did. Eventually, he came to terms with his gayness and expressed it to the pack. They did not take kindly to his sexual orientation.

With no other choice, he gave up his position as alpha and became a lone wolf, destined to roam the world, alone, until one day he might become lucky enough to find the man he was looking for.

But, it was starting to look like that man did not exist.

Everywhere he went, it was always the same. Sure, he'd find an attractive guy or two but never someone worth settling down for. So, he kept searching and searching until he came upon Swansea, a town surrounded by sea and forest.

It was a sleepy little town where the affluent hid from the world, trying to enjoy their wealth, free from the hustle and bustle of the city. People raised their families here. Brought their kids to school in luxury vehicles. Cheered during little league baseball games. And spent Sunday afternoons at the park, flying kites.

Maybe, just maybe, this was where he'd finally find the one.

Clayton sat down and sniffed the air. It was crisp and full of life. He had a good feeling about this place.

A few cars cruised down the street. A biker dressed in tight shorts and a skin-tight shirt hugged his handlebars, enjoying the descent down the hill. At the bottom of that hill, a pair of twins held hands, waiting for the school bus to arrive.

"Well, I might as well start exploring..." Clayton whispered to himself. With his hands in his pockets, he started down the sidewalk.

The sun, now hovering just above the horizon, felt warm against his leather jacket. He adjusted the sleeves and looked at his watch. It was cracked and had stopped working long ago.

It's time for a wardrobe upgrade, he thought. I've been wandering through the woods for way too long.

His clothes were worn thin by his travels. In a way, they gave him a rugged appearance, but they were starting to smell, and he didn't want to go around looking like a bum.

So, he walked into the first coffee shop he saw and slipped into the bathroom. There, he took off his shirt and with a couple of bunched up paper towels, he washed off the dirt from his body. Of course, he would need to take a legitimate shower at some point, but for now, this was the best he could do.

He was just about to finish when a young man opened the door.

Ruben Parker stood there, frozen in place.

He gulped, eyes falling onto Clayton's exposed midsection, carved out with a set of rock-hard abs.

"S-Sorry..." He whispered awkwardly, not quite sure what to say in this sort of situation.

Clayton chuckled. "Why are you apologizing? This is a public bathroom."

"Right..." Ruben nodded, cheeks turning red. "But... can I ask what you're doing?"

"What does it look like I'm doing?"

"Honestly, I have no idea..." Ruben tightened his hold on the bathroom door, half hiding behind it. For some reason, his body was reacting to this handsome stranger. His member twitched in excitement, starting to grow. He bit the inside of his lip, trying to quell the awkward boner. Why was he getting turned on at a time like this?

"Let's just say I'm from out of town and needed a place to freshen up."

"Oh... So, you decided Donut Express would be the best place to do that?"

Clayton shrugged his shoulders. "I just needed a temporary fix." His voice was smooth, gliding through the air and wrapping around Ruben's chest, causing his heart to beat a little bit faster. "So, are you just going to stand there and drool all day or are you going to come in and use the bathroom?"

"Right..." Ruben's face reddened even further. Timidly, he stepped into the bathroom, trying his best to hide his erection from the stranger.

Clayton watched him with interest. The corner of his lip twitched into a knowing smirk.

Then, suddenly, the man's scent hit him like a bullet, piercing through his soul and invigorating him with a frenzied excitement like he had never felt before.

He staggered backward, holding onto the sink to keep steady.

Fuck.

It was absolutely intoxicating.

His pupils dilated, and his heart seemed to beat into oblivion.

What was going on?

The wolf inside him howled with passion wanting to pounce, to sink his teeth into that cute young man and make him scream with lust.

Could it be...?

Was this the man he'd been searching for?

Chapter 2

Clayton emerged from the bathroom feeling a little less gross. His senses were still on high-alert, possessed by the young man that had interrupted his mini shower. If he had been younger, he would have impulsively acted on the desires bubbling inside of him, but he had learned his lesson once before.

He closed his eyes and took a deep breath. No. Now wasn't the time to think of him. He was buried in the past and that was honestly where he should stay.

With a sigh, Clayton walked up to the counter and glanced over the chalkboard menu.

"Can I help you with anything?" A cute, redheaded girl with blue eyes flashed a smile at the traveler.

"I'm just looking for a good cup of coffee."

"Hmm, do you prefer a dark roast or a light roast?"

"Dark. Strong. Flavorful." He leaned in slightly.

The girl blinked, cheeks turning rosy. Her breath caught in her throat. She fell into his eyes, trapped by his dominating gaze. "Um... yeah... that would be our original roast. Should I get you a cup?"

"Please."

"What size?"

"A small is fine."

She nodded. "Can I get a name?"

"Clayton."

"Okay..." She scribbled the name on the side of the cup and handed it over to one of her co-workers. "Coming right up."

Clayton stepped to the side, freeing up the cash register for anyone else who wanted to order a coffee but, at that moment, the shop was relatively empty.

"I hope you don't mind me asking but I've never seen you around before..."

"I'm not from around here. I just rolled in."

"From?"

"Somewhere far, far away."

"If you're trying to sound all mysterious... it's working."

Clayton chuckled. "Let's just say that I like to move around a lot. Exploring the world is what I do."

"But, doesn't that get lonely? I mean, you never get to spend time with your family and friends, right?"

Just then, the bathroom door opened. Ruben stepped out.

Clayton's spine grew rigid as the man's scent permeated the air.

Shit.

He breathed in deep, letting his lungs fill with the sweet aroma.

Mmm.

If only he could take a bite out of him. Surely, that would satisfy his sweet tooth...

But, what was he thinking? Clayton didn't even know that man and yet he was fantasizing about bringing him to bed, pinning him to the mattress, and having his way with him all night long. His hormones raged, making it awkward to stand there. He shifted toward the counter, hiding his erection.

Ruben looked up and spotted the stranger he had caught half naked in the bathroom. Clayton's heart skipped a beat. He bit the inside of his lip to keep himself from moaning aloud. The wolf inside of him whimpered with lust. What was happening to him? Why did he feel this way? He had seen plenty of hot guys before but none of them had affected him quite like this.

The barista waved at her friend. Ruben waved back.

"Do you know him?" Clayton whispered, voice husky with his craving for the young man.

"Yeah, he's my best friend, Ruben." She looked up and tilted her head. "Why do you ask?"

"We just bumped into each other in the bathroom and I was just curious."

"Yep, that's Ruben. He works down at Hugh's. It's a top of the line clothing store for men. Suits. Tuxedos. Dress shirts. They're super expensive so there aren't a lot of people who go in there. I'm kind of jealous. Here I am working my butt off all day and he gets to sit around and read most of the time."

"Hmm, is that so?"

"Yep. Totally not fair."

"Why don't you work there?"

"Oh, trust me, I applied."

Just then, Clayton's coffee was placed on the counter. The girl grabbed it and slid it toward the handsome individual.

"Thanks."

"Oh, and by the way, I'm Beverly. Just... you know... if you were wondering..."

Clayton flashed a smile. "Thank you, Bev." He winked, sending a shiver through her spine.

She blushed darker than ever, heart beating fast. Had that man just flirted with her? The thought made her euphoric and she was already running through everything she'd tell Ruben later that night.

Meanwhile, Clayton sipped his coffee, walking down the street. At first, he wandered aimlessly, familiarizing himself with the town. After all, he'd probably linger for a while. He was tired of traveling all the time. Beverly was right – it was lonely. Clayton longed for a family – for a reason to settle down. After the fight, he had been cast into the role of a lone wolf and while he never complained about it, deep down, he hated being alone. Maybe that's why he was searching so hard for a mate – for someone that could fill the holes in his heart.

Suddenly, he found himself standing in front of Hugh's. He looked up at the glass displays, broadcasting the designer clothes the store had to sell. Clayton pulled out his wallet. He had plenty of money to spend. An odd job here and there meant that he had accrued a small fortune during his travels. People paid good money for someone with his... skill set.

Why was he here?

Leave, he told himself. If you get involved with this man, it'll only end badly.

Clayton knew better than to get involved. And yet, he couldn't walk away. He wrapped his fingers around the door handle and opened it.

Leave, the voice in his head insisted, trying to save him from the heartbreak and headache that was sure to come.

He took a deep breath, trying to decide.

Then, Ruben's scent found its way to his nose and he couldn't possibly leave. Despite his best intentions, despite everything he knew, and despite the voice in his head, he followed his heart instead.

Chapter 3

Ruben was working in the back when he heard the door chime. He hung up the suits that he was supposed to prep for shipment.

In the storefront, he was surprised to find the handsome individual from the bathroom.

What was going on? Was this guy following him or something?

"Um... can I help you?"

"As you can probably tell, I need some new clothes."

Ruben looked at him with a dubious expression. He didn't want to be rude or anything, but this guy didn't look like the kind of person who could afford to shop at Hugh's. Most of the time, old businessmen walked in here with their personal assistants. They'd bark into their phones while the assistant ordered a suit or anything else they might need for their next 'business meeting.' Ruben simply did what he was told. He never asked questions.

But, this time, he couldn't keep his curiosity at bay. "So, um, what's your name?"

"Clayton."

"I'm Ruben." In a professional manner, he held out his hand.

Clayton's eyes seemed to brighten, illuminated by a hidden fire. With a slight smirk playing on his lips, he shook the young man's hand.

At that moment, the world seemed to stop. Both men could feel the electricity in the air. The atoms spasmed all around them. Breathing became impossible. Neither one of them dared to pull away.

Ruben's heart thundered in his chest. His skin tingled. Goosebumps crawled along his arms. What was going on? Why was his body reacting this way?

Again, his inner wolf whimper, this time, yearning to transform and kneel at this man's feet. Ruben blushed. He had always been more of a submissive kind of guy, but it had never gone this far. But, there was just something about this man. Deep down, he knew, that Clayton was an alpha, even if he didn't want to admit it to himself just yet.

Suddenly, he pulled away, trying to compose himself. He shouldn't be having such naughty thoughts about this man. After all, he was just a stranger.

"Anyway, you want some new clothes, then?"

Clayton nodded, watching Ruben's every movement as he crossed the store, heading for the clearance rack.

"Anything you see here will be discounted by 50%. If you ask me, a lot of the stuff here is highly overpriced. These pieces here are our best bargain. Still, I'd probably suggest going down the street to Chloe's. She's our biggest competitor but she has high-quality items for cheap."

"I don't think you're helping the store by sending customers to the competitor." Clayton pointed out.

"I'm just trying to help you save a couple of bucks."

"Don't worry about it." Clayton leaned forward until their bodies were only a few inches apart. "I have plenty of money to spare. Don't worry about the price tag. Just put together a couple of outfits that you think would look good on me. I'll be waiting in the fitting room."

"Oh... um... okay..." Ruben stuttered, not quite sure how to respond. When Clayton disappeared, Ruben shook his head, trying to keep his thoughts innocent but he just couldn't help himself. He undressed Clayton with his mind, starting with his shirt and seeing that perfect set of abs again. Then, he undid his belt, slowly pulling down his pants, revealing his hips. There, a deep 'V' pointed to his crotch where he was no doubt packing quite the member. Ruben licked his lips just thinking about it.

Snap out of it, Ruben chastised himself. You don't even know this guy, so keep your junk in your pants.

Trying his best to focus, Ruben browsed through the store, picking out several outfits. When he was done, he brought them back to the dressing room where Clayton was leaning against a doorway, wearing nothing but his underwear.

Ruben gulped, member coming alive almost immediately. He shifted from foot to foot, embarrassed by the state of his arousal.

"Um... what are you doing?"

"What does it look like I'm doing?" He smirked. "Waiting for you, of course." The way he advanced made Ruben step back, palms sweaty.

What was this guy doing?

There was such a burning in his eyes that he half expected Clayton to pounce on him at any moment. In fact, he almost wanted that to happen. To have this big, strong man pin him against the wall, doing whatever he wanted. Mmm.

But, instead of making a move, Clayton simply grabbed the pile of clothing and disappeared into a dressing room.

Ruben couldn't help but stare at his ass.

Wait.

Why was he so turned on by some dude's butt? Sure, he found guys attractive, but Ruben was pretty sure he was straight. For years, he had tried to get with Bev, his best friend, but for some reason, he could never bring himself to do it. Now, as he stood there, waiting for this man to emerge, a single thought crossed his mind.

Could he be gay?

No, don't be ridiculous, he told himself. But, the more he thought about it, the more logical it became. No one had made him feel this way. His cock struggled for freedom, straining against the rough material of his jeans. He wanted this stranger. He wanted him bad.

But, it would never work. Clayton would run far, far away just as soon as he learned the truth. No one wanted to date a werewolf...

Just then, Clayton stepped out, clad in designer jeans that hung on his hips, a bright blue V-neck shirt, tan shoes, and a matching belt.

Fuck.

He looked sexy as hell.

Ruben stared in utter disbelief. This guy had been handsome before but now... there weren't even words to describe it. He was beyond handsome. He was like some sort of Greek God, crafted out of marble, and brought to life.

Clayton smiled. "What do you think?"

Ruben wet his lips and tried to remember how to breathe. "Amazing."

Chapter 4

"You think so?" Clayton raised an eyebrow in question before walking up to the tri-fold mirror. He stepped onto the pedestal, checking out his newest outfit. "Usually, I try to stay away from bright colors, but I'll have to admit, this looks pretty good."

"Why?"

Clayton shrugged. "Black has always been my color of choice, I guess, especially since..." Suddenly, he stopped thinking, eyes clouding over with pain from the past. "Never mind. I'll take everything."

Ruben's eyes widened. "What?"

"I said, I'll take everything."

"But, you haven't tried everything on yet."

"I don't have to. I trust your sense of style." With these words his eyes swept up and down the young man's body, drinking in his every inch. "I mean, from what I can tell, you're pretty fashionable. Mind giving a clueless guy like me a tip or two?"

"Y-y-you want tips from m-m-me?"

"Of course." Clayton stepped forward, placing a finger underneath his chin, forcing Ruben to look at him. "I like you."

Ruben gulped. "You..." Before he could answer, the front door chimed.

"Hey! Ruben! Are you here? It's me, Bev!"

Quickly, Ruben pulled away. Even as he walked to the front of the store he couldn't shake off the feeling that Clayton was just about to kiss him. The fire in his eyes seemed to try and tell him something but Ruben didn't quite understand what was going on. He could feel the stirring in his heart but too scared to listen, he pushed down these feelings, trying to convince himself that it was all in his head. There was no way that a guy like Clayton could like someone like him.

"Hey, Bev." He waved at his friend, trying to sound as normal as possible but his voice came out high-pitched and flustered.

Beverly cocked her head to the side. "What's wrong?"

"Nothing," Ruben answered quickly. "What are you doing here?"

"My shift ended so I thought I would drop by and keep you company. It's not like you guys get any business here."

"Actually..."

Right on cue, Clayton emerged from the back, still wearing his new outfit and holding the rest of his new clothes in his arms.

"Oh, I see." Beverly smiled at the handsome individual, trying her best to look at him with bedroom eyes. It had been quite a while since she had any luck in the romance department. When she really thought about it, her love life was downright depressing. But, in a small town, there was never very much to choose from. This new guy, however, he was a different story.

"Mind if I ring these out?" Clayton asked, placing the pile of clothing on the counter.

"Of course."

"So, what are you doing here in our tiny little town?" Bev asked, leaning on her elbows, trying to look cute.

Clayton looked at her for a moment before turning his attention, once more, to Ruben. His smell was absolutely intoxicating in such proximity. His nostrils flared as the alpha wolf inside of him raged for release. He wanted nothing more than to shift into his true form and run free with this man. But, how would he react once he learned that he was a werewolf? That was the problem.

"Just passing by. I probably won't stay that long."

Ruben froze.

What?

"Oh..." Beverly frowned. "That's a shame. There's a lot of charm around here. You know, I could show you around sometime."

"I appreciate the offer, but Ruben has already agreed to take me out tonight." Clayton placed his hand on the man's shoulder, squeezing it gently.

Ruben's breath caught in his throat. A shock of electricity coursed through his veins, pulsating through his heart. He shook, nearly losing control. Fuck. If this guy kept teasing him like this, there was no telling what would happen.

"Oh..." Beverly's frown deepened. "Well, maybe next time."

"Yeah, maybe." Clayton nodded.

"Um... so, that'll be $567.99, please..." Ruben interjected, reading the total off the cash register in a semi-robotic voice.

Without a moment's hesitation, Clayton reached into his back pocket and pulled out his wallet. From there, he counted six one-hundred-dollar bills and handed them over.

Ruben was shocked. He didn't expect this man, who had used a donut shop bathroom to 'freshen up,' to have so much money. Nonetheless, he took the cash and handed back the change.

"Perfect." Clayton grabbed his bag. "I'll pick you up once your shift is over."

"O-Okay..." Ruben responded without even thinking about it.

As soon as Clayton was gone, Beverly slammed her hands on the counter. "What was all that about?"

"I... honestly have no idea." Ruben ran his fingers through his hair, trying to get his thoughts straight.

"If I didn't know any better, I'd say that he was flirting with you."

Ruben blushed. "Wait... you really think so?"

"Yeah. He kept looking at you with this fiery expression."

"Really?"

"You mean, you didn't notice?" Beverly shook her head. "You always were oblivious."

"But... do you really think that a guy like that could be... gay?"

"The sexiest ones always are..." She said with a sigh. "He didn't even respond to my flirting."

"You were flirting with him?" Ruben felt a pang of jealousy stab through his heart. He didn't want to admit it, but he was falling for that man. There was something about him that was making his instincts run wild – bringing to life the wolf he always kept dormant. He couldn't explain what it was, but it was there.

"I was trying but we both know how good I am at that..."

"Hey, you'll find someone," Ruben whispered, placing his hand on hers. "I know you will. You're a beautiful girl. Not to mention incredibly smart..."

"I don't need the flattery. It's obvious that Clayton likes you."

Ruben's blush deepened, cheeks turning crimson. "I don't know... why would he like someone like me? I'm a nobody."

Beverly shook her head. "You're more than that, Ruben, and you know it."

Chapter 5

Clayton walked downtown and eventually found an apartment with a 'for rent' sign propped in the window. He called the number scrawled in sharpie and within an hour he had signed a contract, paid the first and last month's, and had been handed over the keys.

As soon as he was alone, he plopped onto the couch. He closed his eyes and immediately fell asleep.

***

In his dreams, he thought of him. The man he had once trusted with his life. He had been young then, blindly following a trickling of lust. But, that was all it was. There was no legitimate feeling beyond the attraction he felt.

And, in the end, it had all been one giant ploy. The man wanted Clayton's position as pack leader. So, he played his cards right, got Clayton to trust him, and then broke his heart into a million little pieces. Clayton was left devastated. His pack rejected him, believing that a gay alpha would only be a weak alpha.

So, he was forced to run away, to roam the Earth as a lone wolf.

In his dreams, he imagined that face, handsome and kind. He had fallen for those eyes that seemed to understand the world. The man held out his hand, beckoning Clayton to take a step forward. Clayton did exactly that. He smiled. The man responded by growling, upper lip twitching, revealing deadly canines.

Suddenly, he shifted, transforming into a giant wolf with fur as black as the night. Before Clayton could respond, those fangs were locked around his windpipe, crushing it until he could no longer breathe. His yellow eyes flashed before he turned his head and furiously ripped out Clayton's throat.

Clayton withered in agony, blood spewing from the wound.

The man licked his chops and walked away, abandoning Clayton forever.

***

Clayton awoke with a start, body covered in a cold sweat.

"Fuck…" He growled under his breath, running his hand along his throat just to make sure it was still intact. "The nightmares just don't want to stop…"

The man had haunted him like a ghost ever since their fight. Clayton had been humiliated by the defeat, leaving the pack wounded, tail between his legs.

Knowing he would simply grow upset if he kept thinking about it, Clayton got up and grabbed his keys. What he needed right now was some fresh air.

Once he was outside, he headed for the woods that circled the town. He was just about to disappear beyond the tree line when a familiar scent made him stop in his tracks.

No.

It couldn't be.

Ever so slowly, he turned around.

Across the street, a well-built man sporting a leather jacket stood there, a diabolical smirk playing on his lips. His smirk deepened as they made eye contact. "It's been a while." He said, voice deep and gravelly.

"Preston…"

"So, you still remember my name." With a confident stride, he advanced, not even bothering to look before he crossed the street.

Clayton remained as still as a stone, feet planted into the ground. He did everything in his power to retain his composure. The last thing he wanted to do was lose his cool in front of this man – at least, not again.

"I've been looking for you for a while now."

"What the hell do you want?" Clayton spat, narrowing his eyes with suspicion. "Haven't you done enough damage?"

Preston chuckled. "You still think I'm a bad guy, don't you?"

"You are." Clayton jabbed his finger into the man's chest, pushing him back. "You fucking destroyed my life just, so you could get a little bit of power. You're a goddamn crook and you know it."

"There's no need for you to hold such a grudge. I won that fight fair and square and you know it."

"Fuck off." Clayton's hands tightened into fists, shaking by his sides. "Now, get out of my goddamn sight before I make you regret it."

"Is that a threat?" Ruben asked, an amused look on his face. "I haven't even told you why I tracked you down."

"I don't care."

"Of course you do. You're dying to know." He stepped forward. The two men squared off, shoulder to shoulder, hip to hip.

"Get the fuck away from me."

"You know, I don't remember you being this rude."

"I was a much better person before you came into my life." Clayton's body itched in anticipation. He was just seconds away from transforming into a werewolf and tearing this man limb from limb – to make him pay for what he had done.

"Oh, come now, things are better this way. You were never meant to be an alpha. I just did what was needed to be done."

Suddenly, Clayton lost his cool. He snarled, grabbed hold of Preston's shoulders, and shoved him into a nearby tree. The trunk cracked under the force of the blow. Leaves fluttered toward the ground.

"Any last words?" Clayton was so angry that every word shook on his lips. He pressed his arm against Preston's throat, remembering his nightmare.

Preston laughed. "You were always so quick to jump into victory. That was your biggest downfall."

"Shut up."

"Make me." Preston challenged, wondering just how far he could push this man.

Clayton was just about to attack when he heard someone running right toward them. He perked his head in the direction of the sound. To his surprise, he saw Ruben.

He was wearing earbuds and looking at the ground.

"Ooo, someone new?" Preston whispered in his ear. "I'd be careful who you trust. Especially when you have three days to get out of this town before the pack goes hunting. If they find you, they aren't going to hesitate to get rid of a mangy mutt like you." And, with that, he wiggled out of Clayton's grasp and disappeared into the forest.

Clayton could do nothing but stand there, torn between chasing after Preston or staying to talk to Ruben.

In the end, his heart decided for him.

Chapter 6

Ruben was so caught up in his run that he didn't even notice the two hulking men growling at each other at the end of the road. Music blasted through his earphones, keeping him motivated as he pushed himself through yet another mile. Ruben had never been particularly strong, but he prided himself on his stamina and speed. In high school, he had been the fastest runner on the track team. As a wolf, he zipped through the forest until the tree trunks blurred against his vision.

He loved running.

Suddenly, he looked up. There was someone standing right in front of him. He tried to skid to a halt, but it was too late. His momentum flung him forward, causing him to collapse into the stranger's body.

Clayton was prepared for this to happen, so he held out his arms and wrapped them around the smaller man, keeping him pinned against his chest. They fell back a few steps but managed to remain upright.

"Are you okay?" Clayton whispered, leaning down until their faces nearly touched. He was tempted, at that moment, to kiss those sweet lips, to do what his body had begged him to do from the beginning, but he held back, doing everything in his power to control the urges that swelled within him.

"Y-Yeah..." Ruben stuttered. He blinked, thinking this was all some sort of dream.

"Are you sure?"

"Yeah..."

Clayton gently placed his hand on Ruben's cheek, looking into his eyes. "I'm glad." He nearly leaned down and kissed the top of his head before he realized what he was doing. The hair on the back of his neck stood on edge. He could tell that he was being watched. No doubt Preston had stuck around. A growl emerged from the back of his throat.

"Clayton...?" Ruben cocked his head in question.

The sound of his name spoken on those sweet lips nearly drove Clayton over the edge. His hormones went wild, threatening to take control. What was happening? Why did he feel this way? He was an alpha. He should have better control over his emotions and yet this man – this stranger – kept affecting him in ways he had never felt before. It made him feel vulnerable and he didn't like that.

And yet, at the same time, he couldn't even imagine letting him go. Now that he had Ruben in his arms, everything seemed to click into place. The vacancy in his heart disappeared, replaced with a warmth that spread through every inch of his body.

"Sorry..."

"Is everything alright?" Even though it seemed weird for Clayton to hold him in the middle of the street, Ruben didn't dare to pull away. He rather liked the feeling of this man's strong arms wrapped around his torso, keeping him safe. He had the odd urge to lay his head on his muscular chest, listen to his heartbeat, and let the day fade away.

"Yeah, I just bumped into an... old acquaintance..."

"And, you weren't very happy to see them?" Ruben guessed.

"Not at all."

"What happened?"

"I don't want to talk about it." Clayton's eyes darkened. "It's something that happened in the past and I rather it stayed there."

"You know, it's not healthy to bottle up your emotions."

Clayton shook his head. "I'm not bottling up my emotions." He stepped back and crossed his arms over his chest. "I just don't like talking about it, is all."

Ruben felt incomplete as soon as Clayton let go of him. A shiver swept through his body, leaving him with a lingering coldness. He could tell, without even knowing this man, that Clayton had suffered a traumatic past. He frowned, wishing there was something he could do to help.

"Anyway..." Clayton broke the silence that had settled around them. He wet his lips, running his fingers through his thick hair. "Did you leave work early or what?"

Ruben nodded. "But, I wasn't going to ditch you or anything... I left a note with the boss with my phone number in case you dropped by."

"I see."

"Honestly, I didn't think you'd come back."

"Why not?"

"Well... because... you're incredibly attractive and I didn't think you'd want to waste your time on someone like me." Ruben whispered, looking down at his running shoes. "Plus... I wasn't entirely sure whether or not you were interested in... you know... guys or not..."

Clayton smirked, amused by Ruben's embarrassment. It was clear to see that this man was one of the innocent ones and Clayton liked that – he liked that a lot – because that meant he had all the opportunity in the world to corrupt him – to turn him into a dirty boy who'd scream his name. Clayton's smirk deepened at the thought.

"Why are you looking at me like that?" Ruben stepped back, bumping into a nearby tree.

Clayton immediately took his opportunity, trapping Ruben against the trunk with his body. In a flash, he had Ruben's wrists pinned above his head, lips dangerously close to his neck. "You really don't give yourself enough credit because as far as I'm concerned, you're irresistible." He nipped at Ruben's earlobe ever so gently, inciting a soft moan that sent a fury raging through his body. If he wasn't careful, he was bound to lose control.

"I..." Ruben gulped, mouth dry. At that moment, it was impossible for him to speak, so he was forced to look at Clayton, eyes wide, heart beating fast, anticipating what was to come.

"What's wrong? Don't you believe me?" Clayton's voice dropped becoming deep and sultry. "Because, if you don't, I can easily prove it to you."

"Prove it to me?" Ruben repeated, brain turning to mush as he became intoxicated by this man's presence.

"Mhm." Clayton slipped his arms around Ruben's body, pulled him close, looked into his eyes, and kissed him.

And, at that moment, Ruben's world exploded in fireworks.

Chapter 7

The kiss continued until Ruben's lungs burned for air. Even then, Clayton continued to kiss him with a fiery passion that consumed every inch of his body.

He clung to Clayton's shirt, steadying himself as his knees grew weak.

Their lips melded into one as their tongues battled for dominance, twisting and turning.

Clayton slammed Ruben into the tree as his lust intensified. He was finding it harder and harder to keep his inner wolf at bay. He growled, teeth nipping at Ruben's bottom lip as naughty fantasies invaded his thoughts. Oh, the things he wanted to do to this man. He'd have him screaming, toes curling, begging for more.

But, before that, he needed to be sure.

The scent was unmistakable – familiar. Ruben was a wolf – one of his kind.

He didn't know why it had taken him so long to figure it out. Maybe he was blinded by the lust.

Nonetheless, if this man truly was a werewolf then, maybe, just maybe, this was the mate he had been searching for all this time.

Just when Ruben thought he was going to pass out, Clayton pulled away. They both panted for breath, looking into each other's eyes as they stood forehead to forehead. "Let's go for a run."

"What?" Ruben furrowed his brows, confused by the sudden request. "You want to go running – now?"

"Why not?" Clayton shrugged.

"You just kissed me..."

"Mhm."

"You kissed me," Ruben repeated, still in a state of shock. He couldn't believe that this handsome individual had kissed him. This had to be some sort of dream. He was sure of it. After all, this sort of thing never really happened.

Clayton chuckled before leaning forward and placing a small peck on his lips. "There, I just kissed you again."

"Why?"

"Why?" Clayton raised an eyebrow in question. "Because, I like you, of course."

"But, how did you know I was gay?"

"I didn't. But, I thought it was worth a shot."

Ruben blushed, trying to make sense of the situation. For most of his life he had tried to convince himself that he was straight. Wasn't that why he had tried so hard to get with Beverly? He wasn't even sure if he liked the kiss. Sure, his lips were tingling, and he felt like he could fly but... did that mean he was gay?

A part of him didn't want to admit it.

And yet, deep down, he always knew he liked men.

"Are you okay?" Clayton asked, pinning a strand of Ruben's hair behind his ear. "I didn't upset you, did I?"

"No." Ruben shook his head. "Not at all... I think... I liked it."

"You think?"

"I've never been with a man before, so this is sort of new to me..." Ruben blushed, feeling shy about his lack of experience. "Don't look at me like that, okay?"

"Hey, it's okay." Clayton placed his hand on Ruben's shoulder, squeezing it gently. "You have nothing to be embarrassed about." He leaned forward and affectionately nipped at his ear.

Ruben giggled. "Do you really like me?"

"I thought the kiss would be enough to prove that to you." Clayton laughed and before Ruben could react, he once again had him pinned against a tree. This time, they were hidden from view. Clayton took his opportunity to slip his hand into Ruben's pants and squeeze his member.

Ruben threw his head back and moaned, feeling a wave of pleasure pulsate through his dick.

Fuck.

Clayton's other hand moved onto Ruben's ass, lifting him off the ground.

Ruben's legs wrapped around the alpha's waist, feet locking together. He slung his arms around his neck as their lips naturally gravitated together.

The kiss started off nice and sweet. Clayton took his time, trying to make Ruben feel good. His hands roamed his slight frame, fingertips traveling along his curves, sending goosebumps rising over his skin.

Ruben moaned. It felt so good.

"You've tempted me from the moment I laid eyes on you," Clayton whispered, voice husky. "I've wanted to take a bite out of you from the start."

Ruben shivered.

"And I'm going to prove just how much I want you…"

"What are you going to do…?"

"You'll see. But, first, you have to do me a little favor."

"Huh?"

"Trust me." Clayton's eyes glowed with such a bright brilliance that Ruben couldn't possibly deny him, no matter what he asked of him. And, for some reason, despite knowing little to nothing about this man, he felt that he could, in fact, trust him. If it came down to it, Ruben would trust him with his life.

"What do you want me to do?"

Clayton smiled, running his fingers through Ruben's hair. "Like I said before, run with me."

Ruben couldn't understand why Clayton had such an urge to go running. He groaned, wishing instead that they could just get on with it. He was becoming so horny that he wouldn't have minded fucking on the forest floor.

"What do you say, can you do that for me?"

"Y-Yes…" Ruben answered without thinking about it.

"Good." Without another word, Clayton shot into the forest.

Ruben stumbled forward, trying his best to keep up. He pumped his arms and focused on his footing. The last thing he wanted to do was trip and make a complete fool of himself. But, it was extremely difficult to focus when all he could think about was the kiss they had just shared. It was his first kiss and something he would never forget.

Gingerly, he reached up and touched his lips. They continued to tingle, as if alive with energy.

"Oh, come on, I know you're faster than that!" Clayton called over his shoulder, trying to edge Ruben on.

Not wanting to be left behind, Ruben pushed himself a little faster, flying over fallen logs and other obstacles with the utmost ease.

As he started to catch up he couldn't help but wonder what was about to happen. He had the sense that today was one of the days that were bound to change his life forever.

Chapter 8

Clayton kept running deeper and deeper into the forest. He knew he was probably venturing into Preston's territory, but he honestly did not care. If Preston wanted a fight, then that's exactly what he was going to get.

Behind him, Ruben was quickly catching up. He was fast – very fast.

Finally, they reached a clearing. Clayton stopped. Ruben did the same, panting for breath. "Where are we?"

"Alone."

"That doesn't answer my question..." Ruben trailed off, losing track of his thought as Clayton advanced toward him with a certain fire burning in his eyes. "Why are you looking at me like that?"

"Because I know your secret."

"My secret?"

"Mhm." Clayton circled around him like a predator about to pounce.

Ruben grew nervous, beads of sweat gathering along the back of his neck. "I-I-I don't know what you mean..."

"Oh, of course, you do." Clayton grinned. "It's the one secret you've never shared with anyone – not even that cute friend of yours, Beverly." He paused. "She has no idea, does she?"

"I..."

"You don't have to keep pretending." Clayton started to take off his clothing, starting with his shirt and then moving to his belt, tossing it onto a nearby rock.

"What are you doing?"

"Taking off my clothes."

"I can see that... but why?"

"You know why." Clayton pulled down his pants, revealing a pair of rather thin underwear that did nothing to hide his growing bulge.

Ruben's eyes gravitated toward this bulge, his own excitement heightening in response. "I..." Again, he found it difficult to speak. His heart beat wildly. No. It couldn't be. Could it...?

To his amazement, as soon as Clayton was fully naked, he started to transform. His arms became hairier and then that hair traveled along the rest of his body, covering him in a thick fur coat.

He let out a silent scream, bones readjusting in size, shape, and density.

Ruben cringed, recognizing the scene all too well. Still, he stood there, unable to believe what he saw with his own eyes.

Clayton was... a werewolf...

Just like him.

When Clayton was done shifting, he emerged as a beautiful silver-furred wolf with emerald green eyes and a hulking body. With a confident step, the beast approached, nuzzling his snout underneath Ruben's hand, gently licking his palm.

"You're... just like me..." Ruben whispered aloud.

Clayton nodded and waited patiently for Ruben to transform as well.

But, Ruben was in a state of disbelief. All his life, he thought that his ability to turn into a wolf was just something he had to experience alone. He had always thought that he was a freak and that's why his parents had abandoned him, leaving him orphaned and afraid.

Again, Clayton licked his palm, trying to encourage him.

"Okay..." Ruben took a step back and started to take off his clothes, piling them on top of a nearby tree trunk.

Clayton watched with hungry eyes as he licked his lips. His tail swayed from side to side, clearly enjoying what he saw.

Once Ruben was naked he took a deep breath and cleared his mind. Only then did the transformation begin. He whimpered, curling up into a ball as a wave of energy shot through his body, giving him the strength he never had while he was a human.

In a flash, he emerged as a small white-furred wolf with dazzling silver eyes that glittered with speaks of gold. He was beautiful.

Clayton couldn't stop himself from getting closer and nipping him on the neck, claiming him as his own.

Ruben moaned, tilting his head back and howling softly. Somehow, being in this form heightened his desire.

The two wolves circled in on one another. They looked into each other's eyes as they moved ever so slowly, as if afraid that at any moment this fantasy would disappear.

Then, suddenly, Clayton lunged forward, pouncing on the smaller wolf.

Ruben let out a yelp of surprise, eyes growing wide. Before he could react, Clayton once again nipped at his neck only this time he allowed his teeth to sink into Ruben's sensitive flesh.

A spasm of pain shot through his body, but it was soon replaced with a brilliant warmth that made him melt under the wolf's embrace. He relaxed and exposed more of his neck, letting the alpha have complete control of his body. Ruben wasn't quite sure what was about to happen, but he didn't care. He wanted this man and he wanted him bad.

Clayton lapped at the wound, causing Ruben's pleasure to intensify. His whole body started to shake.

Mmm.

He was in heaven.

His eyes rolled into the back of his hand as Clayton marked him as his mate.

When he was done, he pulled away and smiled, tongue lolling out of the side of his mouth. Affectionately, he rubbed his head against the smaller wolf's chest.

At that moment, Clayton vowed that he would forever protect Ruben with his life. He had finally found his mate – the one soul he was supposed to share the rest of his life with. The thought made him ecstatic. He no longer needed to roam the world as a lone wolf.

It didn't matter that his pack had rejected him. All that mattered was that he had found the love of his life – the one he had been searching for all this time.

He transformed back to his original form and slipped his fingers through Ruben's fur, holding his head so that he could look into those beautiful gray eyes.

Ruben leaned forward, licking his cheek ever so gently.

Clayton smiled, the holes in his heart finally fully mended, all thanks to this man he barely knew. If this was just the beginning he could only imagine how good things were sure to become.

"I love you." He whispered, speaking from the soul, and finally listening to the instincts he had always tried to keep dormant.

Chapter 9

Ruben's ears twitched. Had he heard correctly?

Clayton loved him?

No.

That couldn't be.

It didn't make any sense. They had only just met. Sure, they were attracted to each other and sure, they were both werewolves, but wasn't saying 'I love you' jumping the gun just a tad bit? And yet, Ruben couldn't help but feel the same way.

There was just something about this man. It was like he was the missing puzzle piece of Ruben's life, suddenly bringing the world into perfect clarity. It didn't make any logical sense, but, he loved this man too.

Slowly, he transformed back into his human form.

As soon as he did, Clayton lost all control. He grabbed his newly acquired mate and brought him to the ground, pinning him by the shoulders. Without an ounce of hesitation, he kissed Ruben's lips, letting all the fiery passion he felt in his soul come to the forefront.

Immediately, Ruben's cock throbbed in response, getting harder and harder with each passing second. Soon, it stood at attention, poking Clayton who simply took it into his hand and started to stroke it up and down, taking his time and teasing the young wolf. He rolled his thumb over the tip until Ruben bucked his hips into the air, begging for more.

Clayton chuckled. "Do you like that?"

Ruben couldn't even think of a response. His mind had turned to mush. All he could do was roll his hips into the air, cock twitching with pleasure, balls tightening. Somehow, he was already getting close to orgasm and it had only been a few minutes.

But, Clayton wasn't about to let the fun end so soon. He flipped his lover, positioning him on all fours. He grabbed a fistful of Ruben's hair and yanked his head back.

Ruben yelped, back arching.

Slowly, Clayton trailed his lips along the side of Ruben's neck, searching for his sweet spot. Once or twice his tongue darted in the direction of the mating mark clearly imprinted on Ruben's neck, just below the ear. When he did so, wave after wave of pleasure rolled into Ruben's body. He moaned, body squirming.

"Mmm, how much do you want me?" He whispered, nipping at his earlobe. "Beg for it, Ruben. Tell me just how bad you want to feel my cock deep inside of you."

Ruben shivered. His lips felt like they were incredibly dry, the lack of moisture causing them to fuse together. Between his legs, his cock threatened to explode. He wanted nothing more than to have sex with this man but, at the same time, he struggled to express his lust, to put it into words, because what he felt in that moment was something carnal – instinctual – something that his inner wolf had always yearned for.

"Go on, beg." Clayton insisted, voice dominant. Gently, his lips traveled from his lover's neck down to his spine. He lingered on the lower back while his fingertips danced along his sides, causing him to shiver even further. "Just say the word and I'll make you feel like no one else has. I'll rock your whole world. Trust me."

"Please..." Ruben's bottom lip quivered. He dug his fingers into the soft dirt underneath his hands. "I want you... so bad..."

"I don't think I believe you." Clayton moved behind his lover, placing his hands on his hips. His cock, massive in size, poked against Ruben's entrance, teasing him with it. "Do you think you could take a cock like mine?" He whispered, planting kisses on his shoulder blades.

Ruben nodded. "Please..." He begged once more. "I want to feel you plunge inside of me. I want to feel your cock fill every inch of my hole. Please... make me yours."

Clayton grinned. Without a doubt, this was his true mate, the one wolf that could complete him.

Wanting to make the experience pleasurable for his inexperienced lover, Clayton wet one of his fingers in his mouth before slowly slipping it into Ruben's tight little whole.

Ruben immediately became tense, curling his toes and arching his back.

"Shh, just relax. I'll go easy on you. I promise." As he said this, he began to move his finger in and out, taking a slow pace that quickly grew pleasurable.

Once Ruben started to moan, he moved his finger a little bit faster, twisting it this way and that, trying to stimulate his mate.

Soon, Ruben had his head thrown back, howling at the moon that was slowly starting to make its way into the sky. He shook with pleasure wishing that Clayton's finger could be replaced with something else – something much, much better. He bit his lip, holding back a scream.

"That's it..." Clayton smirked. "I want to hear you howl. I want to hear you shout my name." Suddenly, he shoved in another finger, pumping it hard and fast for a moment before bringing down the pace.

Ruben groaned. "Please..."

"Please what?" With his other hand, Clayton began stroking Ruben's cock. Occasionally, he'd give his balls a squeeze, just making him moan a little louder.

Ruben felt like he was losing his mind. He didn't know how much more of this he could take. Already, pleasure coursed through his every vein making him feel more alive than ever.

Clayton stroked him even harder, feeling Ruben's member becoming stiff. He added yet another finger, fucking his virgin hole with all three, trying to loosen him up for the main event. "Just relax, baby, I'm going to make you feel so good." Gently, he ran his fingers through Ruben's hair, once again pulling on it until he was forced to look at the sky.

Ruben bit his lip, instinctually knowing what was about to happen next.

Clayton positioned himself behind his lover and took the plunge.

Chapter 10

Clayton only managed to penetrate a few inches before he was met with resistance. "Fuck, you're tight." He growled, digging his claw-like nails into Ruben's hips, adjusting his grip.

With another thrust of his hips, he managed a few more inches.

Ruben screamed in a mixture of pain and pleasure. "Fuck!"

"What's the matter, baby?" Clayton ran his hand along Ruben's body, eventually finding one of his sensitive nipples. He took it between his fingers, rolling his thumb around the hard, little nub.

Ruben's moans turned him on more than anything else causing his cock to twitch inside his mate.

"Just relax..." He cooed, gently sucking on the side of his neck, lapping his tongue against the mark that bound them together.

Ruben melted against the pleasure, body relaxing, making it easier for Clayton to slip inside of him. This time, he managed to go all the way.

He stopped, letting his body adjust to the situation. Clayton couldn't believe how incredibly tight his mate was and Ruben couldn't believe how unbelievably massive his lover was. It felt like Clayton was bound to rip him in half at any moment. He clung to the ground, trying to steady himself.

Suddenly, Clayton pulled out, nearly taking out his dick completely. He hesitated for a moment before slipping in once more, letting Ruben feel every single inch slip inside of him.

Ruben moaned, back arching.

Clayton couldn't help but slap his ass and watch it bounce around his cock. He slapped it again, turning the skin a rosy red.

Ruben howled.

Turn on, Clayton started to move his hips in a steady rhythm. Soon, he was fucking Ruben nice and slow, taking his time so the moment could last.

"Fuck..." Ruben growled under his breath.

"Cum for me," Clayton commanded as he ran his nails along Ruben's back, leaving behind soft red lines.

Ruben moaned louder than ever, body shaking. His balls were so tight that he felt like they were about to explode and yet, he continued to stifle his orgasm, wanting this moment to last forever. It felt so good. Too good. And, he didn't want it to end.

"Please... fuck me harder..." Ruben was already addicted. No one had ever made him feel this way. He howled louder and louder, telling the whole world had amazing he felt.

Encouraged by his mate's pleasure, Clayton grabbed hold of Ruben's hair and started going to town. He pounded into the tight, little hole harder and harder. Their balls started to slap together, echoing through the forest.

He pushed Ruben's head down so his ass was even further in the air. Growling, he kept nipping at his lover's body, leaving behind various love marks. Clayton grunted, cock twitching, just on the cusp of orgasm.

"Cum for me!"

This time, Ruben could no longer hold back. His cock exploded, spewing string after string of sticky cum onto the grass beneath him. He panted for breath, arms and legs growing weak, making it extremely difficult for him to support his lover's weight.

But, it didn't take long for Clayton to orgasm as well. After a few more thrusts, he shot his load into his lover before slowly pulling out and collapsing to the ground.

Ruben fell into his arms and he gently held him in his embrace. "That was amazing..." He whispered, kissing the top of his head. "And, you want me to believe that you've never been with someone before?"

"I mean..." Ruben blushed crimson. "... it's true. You were my first. Just not."

"Well, how does it feel?" Clayton asked as he slowly ran his fingertips along Ruben's spine.

Ruben smiled, nuzzling his head into Clayton's chest. A sense of warmth and serenity washed over him. It seemed that so long as he remained in Clayton's arms that nothing bad could ever happen to him. He'd be safe forever.

"It feels amazing..." He finally answered. "You know, I never thought I'd find someone, being a wolf and all. I didn't know there were others like me."

"Oh, there's a lot of other werewolves. Trust me."

"Then, why aren't you with them?"

Clayton's expression darkened. "They rejected me." He took a deep breath and looked into Ruben's loving eyes. Ruben deserved the truth and that was exactly what he was going to give him. "My father was the alpha of my pack. So, when he died, I was the next in line."

Ruben listened intently to the story, all while his head rested on Clayton's chest, listening to his heartbeat.

"But, at the time, I was with someone. A man. No one particularly approved of me being with him. You see, if I'm gay then that means I can't have pups which means no future alphas to take over the pack. But, I thought this man would stick by my side... and in the end, he betrayed me. He did everything he could to slander my good name just so he could become the alpha himself. And so, the pack abandoned me, forcing me to live as a lone wolf. I became hateful against my own kind, but I knew if I could only find my true mate the one wolf in this world that belonged to my soul that I'd find purpose again. And here I am, with you." With these words, Clayton kissed the top of his head and smiled.

"I didn't think I would ever be that special to someone..." Ruben whispered.

"Trust me, you're the most precious person in the world to me." Clayton tightened his arms around his lover.

"I love you..." Ruben spoke those words without even thinking about it. His eyes widened in disbelief. His heart skipped a beat. Could it be that he really did love this man? That their love could stem from some invisible force of attraction he did not understand?

Clayton smiled once more and kissed him.

And, at that moment, Ruben knew without a doubt that this man was the love of his life.

Chapter 11

The two men fell asleep in the soft grass. Clayton kept Ruben cocooned in his embrace, threatening to never let him go.

Ruben rested his head on the crook of Clayton's shoulder, a groove that seemed like it was made just for him. He smiled, snuggling nice and close, feeding off the warmth that radiated from Clayton's body. He hadn't felt this happy in years.

They both dreamt pleasant dreams as the moon crept along the sky and eventually faded toward the horizon, replaced by the sun. As the landscape was painted with bright oranges, the two men continued to sleep, much too content to wake up.

But, all around them, yellow eyes began to emerge from the thicket of trees. They watched the couple with hungered interest. A few of them were ready to pounce right then and there but their leader held them at bay.

Preston circled around the clearing, waiting for the perfect moment to attack. It pissed him off that Clayton had finally found his true mate. A mutt like him didn't deserve such happiness. Clayton was weak. A nobody. A wolf who should be ashamed of his status as an alpha. He was a failure and Preston was ready to end him once and for all.

A couple of sparrows shot out from their nest and flew into the air. They spiraled toward the sun before diverging into different directions – one to the left and one to the right. As they disappeared into the surrounding forest, they sounded their morning call. In turn, other birds started to emerge from their nests, filling the woodland with an orchestra of different chirps.

Clayton stirred, ears twitching. He woke up, greeted by the bright sun starting its day. He groaned and tried to roll over only to remember that he still held Ruben in his arms.

Suddenly, his memory of last night came crashing into him. He smiled. So, that hadn't been a dream after all. He had truly found his mate.

With a smile on his face, he kissed Ruben's cheek.

Ruben scrunched his nose and tried to bury his face in Clayton's cheek.

Clayton chuckled. "What are you doing?"

"Five more minutes," Ruben mumbled.

Clayton started to shower his lover's face with kisses.

Ruben couldn't help but giggle. He curled up into a little ball.

"Oh, is someone ticklish?" Clayton smirked before he started to tickle his mate, trying to find his most ticklish areas. As soon as he started to tickle Ruben's side, he lost all control, curling up and laughing, trying to get away. But, Clayton overpowered him, pinning him down with one hand while the other continued the assault.

"Please!" Ruben gasped for air, laughing so hard that he had begun to cry. "I can't breathe..."

Clayton continued for a moment longer before stopping. There was a bright smile on his face as he looked down at his mate. "I love you."

"I love you, too." It felt so easy to say those words as if he had waited all his life to say them.

They lingered on the grass for a little while longer before Clayton got up and gathered their clothes. "We should get dressed."

Ruben nodded, tossing on his underwear. "I should probably get to work... what time is it anyway?"

Clayton shrugged. "I have no idea. Early. The sun isn't fully out yet."

Once they were fully dressed, Clayton grabbed Ruben's hand, about to leave the forest when the hair on the back of his neck prickled. He stopped, sniffed the air, and froze in place.

No.

It was too late.

They were already surrounded.

Now that he was aware of it, he could see the countless eyes peeking out from the tree line.

He grabbed Ruben and pushed him behind his back, trying to keep him safe.

"What are you doing?"

"The wolf pack... they've found me."

Ruben gulped. "What do you mean they found you?"

"They're here." Clayton kept circling around, keeping his senses alert in case any one of them decided to jump forward and make a move. He held his breath, trying to remain calm. Right now, all that mattered was keeping Ruben safe.

"Where did you think you were going?" Preston finally stepped forward, a smug look on his face. "You should have known better than to fool around on my territory."

"You were never the owner of this land," Clayton growled. "Another pack used to live here."

Preston laughed. "You're right. They used to live here."

"What have you done to them?" Clayton demanded, feet firmly planted in the ground, refusing to budge.

Behind him, Ruben felt his heart beating so fast that it threatened to beat out of his chest. He had no idea what was about to happen, but something told him that whatever it was, it wouldn't end well. He could feel the hatred sizzling between these two men. Could this be the man Clayton had told him about? The one that had betrayed him? Just the thought got Ruben's blood boiling. If only he was stronger then he wouldn't hesitate to sink his teeth into his neck and rip out his fucking throat.

Ruben was surprised by his own anger. His fists shook. He wanted nothing more than to make this man pay for all the pain he caused his mate.

"They've simply joined my ranks," Preston answered with a shrug. "They saw reason."

"You've taken away their home – their autonomy."

"Yeah, maybe I killed their alpha but so what? Wolves kill each other all the time. Why should werewolves be any different?"

"You disgust me."

"You only say that because you're scared. You've always feared me. Face it, you're just as weak now as you were then." He stepped forward. "Which is why I won't feel a drop of remorse when I finally end you and rid the world of your filth."

And then, something snapped inside of Ruben that sent him flying forward.

Chapter 12

Ruben transformed into a wolf in midjump. He growled causing his top lip to curl, exposing his teeth, trying to look menacing.

He stalked forward.

Preston laughed. "Oh, this is too good. You can't fight your own battles, so you send this runt to do the fighting for you. That's too good." He shook his head. "Really, I thought you were better than that, at least."

Suddenly, Ruben lunged forward, grabbing hold of Preston's ankle. He bit down with all his strength, trying to snap the bone to no avail. Nonetheless, he tasted blood in his mouth as he severed Preston's skin.

The crook kicked out his leg, sending the lesser wolf flying through the air.

Ruben collided with a nearby tree trunk, whimpering on impact.

Preston was just about to attack and end his worthless life when a flash of silver shot in his direction.

A second later, Clayton had tackled him to the ground, snarling like a wild animal. He was so enraged that he had completely given himself up to the wolf inside.

Just in time to save himself, Preston threw a punch. It landed squarely on Clayton's snout.

He stumbled off his enemy and wobbled on his feet.

"You really shouldn't have done that because now I'm angry and you really wouldn't like me when I'm angry." Preston wiped the blood from his nose. "And, have you dumb fucks forgotten that you're surrounded? All I have to do is snap my fingers and the entire pack will come running, tearing you both limb from limb. But, I'm better than that. I rather do the job myself." Without another word, he shifted into his wolf form.

Preston was massive, hulking above all the other wolves that had emerged from the tree line and were now closing in, forcing a tight circle, making it impossible for either Ruben or Clayton to escape.

Clayton growled, trying desperately to think of a way out of this. He glanced back at Ruben who looked petrified. No matter what, he had to save his mate, even if it meant sacrificing his own life.

He stepped forward, squaring up to his ex-lover. The two wolves growled, sizing each other up.

Preston jumped forward. Clayton jumped back.

They continued to tiptoe around each other.

Suddenly, Clayton tripped, stumbling forward.

Preston took the opportunity to grab Clayton by the neck, sink his teeth into his flesh, and toss him across the clearing.

Clayton hit the ground hard. A cracking sound echoed through the air, causing Ruben to flinch. No doubt, some of Clayton's ribs had cracked. Ruben desperately wanted to help but he was frozen in place, too scared to move. What was he supposed to do? What would happen if Clayton lost this fight?

Preston shot forward, grabbing Clayton by the leg and dragging his body like a rag doll.

Clayton howled as red-hot pain engulfed his entire leg. It felt like Preston was about to rip it right out of the socket.

He tried to struggle but no matter what he did, he couldn't free himself.

No.

This couldn't be happening.

He couldn't lose to this man – again.

With newfound energy, he managed to get up. There was blood dripping from his wounds but nonetheless, he stood his ground, eyes blazing with hatred.

Preston cackled, amused by the wolf's determination but it didn't matter. This would all be over soon.

He growled, lunging into the final attack.

Clayton dodged and grabbed Preston by the neck, teeth locking around his windpipe.

Preston struggled, clawing at his sides, drawing blood that clotted around Clayton's fur.

Suddenly, Ruben joined the fight, jumping on Preston's back and doing everything he could to help, nearly ripping off Preston's ear in the process.

The alpha bucked, throwing Ruben off. With a swipe of his paw, he injured Clayton just enough to cause him to fall back. Taking his opportunity, he turned and disappeared into the forest, howling into the sky, vowing to return.

Clayton panted for breath. The two wolves looked at each other, lucky to be alive.

Ruben nuzzled his mate, silently asking if he was okay.

But, Clayton had lost a lot of blood and continued to lose blood. Too weak to stand, he collapsed. His body shook, transforming back into a human. He was naked and cold, body lacerated with deep cuts.

Quickly, Ruben shifted back as well. He had managed to emerge from the fight relatively unscathed, save for a few cuts and bruises. "Clayton... oh my god..." He rushed to his lover's side, eyes nearly bugging out of his head.

"Are... are... you okay?" Clayton found it difficult to breathe. His neck was bleeding more than any other injury to his body.

"Don't talk," Ruben spoke quickly and grabbed his shirt, tying it around Clayton's neck, trying to stop the bleeding. "We have to get you to a hospital. You're losing a massive amount of blood." The words spilled out of his mouth like a torrent. He was on the verge of panicking. He didn't even want to fathom the possibility of losing Clayton.

No.

Whatever he did, he needed to save him.

"You... can't..." Clayton croaked. "They would know... that... I'm a... werewolf..." He struggled to say this simple sentence, lips quivering from the effort. And then, it was all too much for him. He fainted, body growing limp in Ruben's arms.

"Clayton!" He shouted.

No response.

"Clayton... please... you can't leave me." He shook Clayton by the shoulders but still, there was no response. Angry tears stung at his eyes as he feared the worst. He clung at Clayton's shirt as the tears flowed down his cheeks. Slowly, he leaned down, resting his head on Clayton's chest. To his relief, his heart continued to beat. That meant, there was still a chance.

He grabbed Clayton and slung his arm over his shoulder, dragging him out of the forest, calling on every ounce of strength he had.

As they walked, they left behind a trail of blood, making it incredibly easy for the pack to track them down.

Ruben just prayed they'd be left alone for a while but deep down he knew they'd be back, sooner rather than later.

Chapter 13

Clayton woke up sometime later in an unfamiliar bed. He opened his eyes, staring at a ceiling decorated with little plastic stars that were faintly green in color. Glow in the dark, he guessed.

He blinked.

"You're awake." A female voice broke the silence.

He turned his head but doing so caused a stabbing pain to penetrate through his temples. Not only that but there was a thick collar wrapped around his neck making it difficult to move his head left and right.

What was going on?

"Careful." She placed her fragile hand on his. "You don't want to hurt yourself."

To Clayton's surprise, the girl happened to be the same one from the coffee shop – Beverly – at least that's what he thought her name was. His memory was a bit hazy like someone had taken a sledgehammer to his head and scrambled everything he kept stored there.

"What happened?" He asked, wetting his lips just enough to speak those words. His voice came out as a cracked wheeze.

"I don't really know. One second, I'm reading a book on the couch, enjoying some Sunday morning tea and the next Ruben comes barging in with you in his arms. Blood everywhere."

At the mention of his lover's name, Clayton's eyes shot open.

Ruben!

What had happened to him? Was he okay?

"Don't worry. He's fine. And, evidently, you are too, thanks to him."

"Where is he?"

"Taking a nap. He's been up all night taking care of you." She grabbed a wet cloth and placed it on his forehead.

Clayton sighed, enjoying the cool relief.

"You have a pretty nasty fever. I've been trying to bring it down but for some reason, it won't budge."

Clayton didn't dare to tell her that werewolves had a naturally higher body temperature than humans. It was best if she didn't know. As far as he could tell, Beverly was a kind-hearted soul and he wanted to keep it that way. If she learned about the monsters that lurked in her world, she would never look at it the same way again.

Just then, Ruben appeared in the doorway. His eyes widened as soon as he saw that Clayton was awake. He flew forward, wrapping his arms around his lover, crying happily. "I'm so glad you're okay..."

Even though it pained him to do so, Clayton wrapped his arms around Ruben's slender torso, pulling him close. "What happened?"

Ruben bit his lip, glancing sideways at Beverly.

She sighed. "Okay, I get it, you want me to leave."

"Sorry, Bev."

"Don't worry about it. I know you'll tell me sooner or later." With that she got up and left the room, closing the door behind her.

As soon as they were alone, Clayton took Ruben's face into his hands and pulled him into a kiss. Their lips melted together, yearning for one another.

Ruben shivered.

Clayton felt his strength reemerge.

Finally, they pulled away, looking into each other's eyes, glad that they had both survived.

Ruben took Clayton's hand and held it tightly. "How do you feel?"

"Like shit."

Ruben frowned. "I'm sorry... I tried to do everything I could. When you said I couldn't take you to the hospital, I panicked. So, I brought you here. Bev and I are both studying to become nurses. She's much better at it than I am so you should really thank her for your recovery..."

"You're the one who carried me. The one that saved my life..." Clayton whispered. "If it weren't for you, I'd be dead."

Ruben shuddered at the thought. "I don't want to think about that..."

"Okay." Clayton gently ran his fingers through Ruben's hair. "Everything's going to be okay. I promise."

For some reason, Ruben didn't quite believe him. There was a growing knot forming in his stomach that only became tighter and tighter. "He's going to come back, isn't he?"

Clayton hesitated to answer but, in the end, he nodded. "Yes."

"Who is he?"

"Preston."

"Is he the one who betrayed you?"

Again, Clayton nodded. "And now, he wants to finish me."

"I won't let him," Ruben growled.

"I don't want you to get involved. This is my fight."

"I'm not going to let you do this alone."

"I don't want you to get hurt." Clayton insisted. "You don't know what he's capable of. He's a tyrant and he must be stopped."

"You and I both know that going after him would be nothing less than a suicide mission."

"Ruben, you're not going to stop me."

"And, you aren't going to stop me from helping you."

"I can't let you do that." Clayton took Ruben's hand, lacing their fingers together and bringing them to his chest. "I can't stand the thought of losing you. If something were to happen to you, I'd never be able to forgive myself."

Ruben shook his head. "We have a better chance if we stick together. Don't be stubborn for the sake of your own ego."

Clayton shook his head. "I have to do this... alone." He was angry at himself for losing. He was an alpha – one of the most powerful werewolves – and yet, he couldn't beat some lowlife. It was despicable. Pathetic.

"Please... don't do this..." Ruben pleaded with him, but it was too late, Clayton had already made up his mind.

As soon as he had fully healed, he would hunt down that bastard and make him pay for all the pain he had caused. He would regret the day he ever betrayed him.

Ruben frowned, telling by the hatred in Clayton's eyes that he was already planning his defense. With a sigh, he started to unravel some of the bandages around his leg. The wounds from a few days ago already looked much better.

Soon, Beverly would start to question his accelerated healing process and Ruben would be forced to tell her the truth.

Chapter 14

Once Clayton was given another dose of pain medicine, he fell into a deep slumber.

Ruben ran his fingertips along his cheeks and sighed. Only a few days ago, his life had seemed so normal and now everything was being turned upside down. This dashing young man had come into his life, changing everything.

He stepped out of the bedroom and headed for the kitchen. There, he found Beverly standing in front of the kettle, waiting for the water to boil. She looked up, apple in hand, taking a bite.

Ruben didn't say a word as he opened the pantry and pulled out a bag of beef jerky – his favorite snack.

"So, when are you going to tell me what's going on with Clayton?"

Suddenly, the jerky felt like it had lodged itself in his throat. He struggled to swallow, his mouth becoming dry. This was it. The moment he had been dreading his entire life. Somehow, he had managed to keep his secret from Beverly despite being best friends with her since childhood. Now, he was about to reveal that he was some sort of monster. How would she react?

"It's a long story."

"It's my day off, I've got enough time. Besides, our biology exam got postponed until next Friday, so we have time to study, too."

Ruben was so caught up in his own personal drama that he hadn't even thought about his biology exam. Right now, the digestive system and the endocrine system were the furthest things from his mind.

The electric kettle went off with a ding.

Beverly grabbed a mug and poured the hot water over a tea bag. "Do you want any?"

"No, thanks."

"Are you sure? It'll calm your nerves. I'd suggest you drink something, but I know alcohol isn't your thing."

Ruben started to pace back and forth, trying to figure out the best way to tell her the truth.

"What are you doing?" Beverly asked, raising an eyebrow in question.

"I don't know where to start, Bev. I want to tell you everything but at the same time, I'm extremely scared of how you'll react."

Beverly placed a hand on his shoulder and smiled. "I'm your best friend. So, no matter what, I'll stick by your side. Remember that."

"Even if... say... I was a... werewolf..." Ruben's whisper was so low that Beverly barely heard what he said.

She smiled.

Ruben cocked his head in confusion. That was not the response he had expected.

"I already knew that."

"You what?" He spat.

"I've known for a while now." Her smile deepened.

"What? How?"

"You weren't very good at hiding it." She said with a shrug. "I mean, you'd tell me you were going for a run in the middle of the night to 'clear your head' and then I'd see you transform through the back window. I thought about confronting you, but I figured you wanted to keep it a secret."

Ruben stood there, mouth agape, unable to believe that Beverly had known he was a shifter all along and somehow, she still stuck around.

"And, when were you going to tell me you were gay?"

"Don't tell me that you knew about that too..." Ruben said, slightly embarrassed.

"For a long time. Probably since middle school, honestly."

"What? How?" He repeated.

"Trust me, it's obvious. You would try to flirt with me to seem 'normal' but I could always tell that you were never interested. Besides, we were always into the same guys. Even now, you ended up with the hottie I wanted."

His eyes widened. "You mean... you like Clayton."

"I mean, I was attracted to him, sure. Who wouldn't be? The guy's smoking hot. But now that I know you two are an item, I'll be sure to keep my eyes to myself." She said with a wink. "Oh, and about that, did you two...?"

"Beverly!" Ruben exclaimed. "I don't really think – "

"Sorry, I didn't mean to pry." She giggled. "There's no need to get so flustered."

There was a momentary silence.

Beverly sipped on her tea.

Ruben stood there, not quite sure what to say. "So, despite knowing who I really am, you still want to be my friend?"

"Of course." She smiled. "But, only on one condition."

"Oh?" Ruben cocked his head in question. "And, what's that?"

"I want to see what you look like up close."

"You want me to transform into a wolf?"

She nodded. "Mhm."

"But, won't you be scared?"

"Scared?" She laughed. "Come on, when have I ever feared anything. Or should I remind you that whenever you squeal like a baby because there's a spider in your room that I'm always the one to come to your rescue?"

Ruben blushed. "Hey... there's no need for a low blow."

She smirked. "Well, go on then, I want to see the big bad wolf."

"I'm really nothing to look at it."

"Stop being so modest and just transform already."

"Okay, close your eyes, then?"

"Why?"

"Because I have to get undressed."

Beverly sighed. "It's not like I've never seen you naked, you know."

"Yeah, but, I'm taken now."

She smiled. "You really like him, don't you?"

"More than you know..." Ruben whispered. He waited for Beverly to close her eyes before he started to undress, piling his clothes on the kitchen table. Once he was naked, he started to transform.

Beverly couldn't help but sneak a quick peek. She gasped, watching as his body shifted into that of a white-furred wolf. Her eyes nearly bulged out of her head. "Whoa..." Hesitantly, she stepped forward, holding out her hand.

Ruben nuzzled her palm.

"You're so soft!" She said with a smile. "And your fur... it's so white."

Ruben seemed to smile at her, tongue lolling out the side of his mouth. He got up on his hind legs and kissed her cheek.

Maybe, just maybe, this would all work out in the end...

At least, he hoped so.

Chapter 15

Two weeks later.

Clayton, by now, was fully healed. His skin showed no sign of his fight with Preston save for a small scar across the length of his neck.

He had been on high alert since the attack, half expecting his ex-lover to ambush him or his mate at any moment but things, for the most part, were quiet – too quiet. Clayton was suspicious of everything, scared that all he needed to do was blink and catastrophe was sure to strike.

Beside him, Ruben was fast asleep. He didn't seem to have such concerns. With his head on Clayton's chest, he smiled to himself, dreaming pleasant dreams.

Clayton gently ran his fingers through his hair, trying not to wake him.

Suddenly, he heard a twig snap outside the window. He tensed, listening closely for any other sounds. Although faint, he could hear approaching footsteps.

He took a deep breath and the smell of wet dog permeated the air.

Fuck.

They had finally arrived.

He shook Ruben by the shoulders. "Ruben."

Ruben groaned and rolled over, hiding his face in the pillow. "What?" He grumbled.

"We have to go."

"Go? What are you talking about? It's two in the morning..." He turned over, glaring at his lover. "And nothing in the world is going to get me out of this bed."

"They're here." Clayton insisted. "We have to go. It's not safe. Preston brought the whole pack. There's no way we can beat them."

Ruben sat up, suddenly awake. He could sense their presence, slowly closing in around the house. He shivered with fright, clinging to the sheets.

"Come on." Clayton grabbed his hand, about to pull him out of bed.

"No."

Ruben's response came as a shock. Clayton looked at him, eyebrows furrowing together in confusion. "What do you mean no? We don't have time for this. We need to run now."

"No. Don't you get it? If we keep running, then that's all we'll ever do. We need to face this, once and for all. This is my home and I'm not leaving." He said with such conviction that it fueled Clayton with the resolve he needed to lay down his life for this man – to protect the home he so loved – to make the world safe for the two of them so they could finally start a life together like he had always dreamed of.

But, before they could decide on a plan of action, there came a blood-curdling scream from Beverly's room.

Ruben's eyes widened in concern. The two men looked at each other for a moment before rushing out of the room and down the hall.

They barged into Beverly's room where Preston was holding her hostage, arm wrapped around her neck, tightening his hold with each passing second.

Desperately, Beverly clawed at his arm, trying to set herself free, but she was no match for a werewolf. "Please..." She begged.

Preston shook his head. "Humans are rather pathetic, don't you think? They are always begging for their lives."

"And you'll be doing the same if you don't let her go." Clayton stepped forward. "You've tormented me, and I'm done taking your shit. This ends tonight."

"Is that a threat?" Preston asked with a smirk playing on his lips. "I think I might have struck a nerve."

"Look, I know you have your whole pack surrounding the house, but they don't need to get involved. This is between you and me. If you really do think that you're better than me then let's prove it once and for all. We'll fight – this time, to the death. Whoever wins becomes the rightful alpha."

Preston's smirk deepened. "I like the way you think. But, I don't particularly feel like fighting you tonight. Instead, I think I'll be taking this one back with me. I'll keep her safe until the fight, don't you worry."

This time, Ruben stepped forward, growling in response. "Don't you dare hurt her."

"Aww, and the puppy has decided to join the fight. How cute."

"You bastard." Beverly snapped. "You're insane if you think I'm going anywhere with an asshole like you."

"Feisty. I like that."

Clayton rushed forward but before he could save Beverly, a couple of wolves jumped in front of him, growling viciously. There were too many of them. If he tried to pick a fight, then someone was bound to get hurt. As much as he hated it, he would be forced to play by Preston's rules.

He retreated. "What do you want?"

"You'll meet me at the clearing tomorrow at noon. We'll fight, one on one, but feel free to bring your little boyfriend if you want him to witness your death."

Clayton ground his teeth together.

"Until then, I'll be keeping her and don't try anything or else your little friend won't live to see the light of day. You hear me? If you want, go ahead and call my bluff but I wouldn't risk if it I were you."

"You're a coward, Preston." Clayton shook with anger. He wanted to do something – anything – to help Beverly. The fear in her eyes broke his heart. And yet, what was he supposed to do? If he attacked, she was as good as dead – they all were.

"Call me what you want but I'm the one holding all the cards in my hands. So, you better fold before you get yourself in trouble." With that, he jumped out the window with Beverly in his arms.

Ruben and Clayton rushed forward, watching them disappear into the woods.

"No!" Ruben screamed, running his fingers through his hair in frustration while he paced around the room. "This can't be happening. What is he going to do to her?"

Clayton placed a hand on his shoulder. "Ruben, calm down."

"Calm down? How do you want me to calm down when my best friend has been kidnapped by a maniac?"

"I'll fix this," Clayton promised. "I'll get her back."

Chapter 16

"You're not really going through with this, are you?" Ruben asked, keeping pace with Clayton as he jogged through the woods.

"What choice do we have?" Clayton stopped, looking into the eyes of his love. "That bastard took Beverly and I know how much she means to you. Besides, I owe her my life after all. It's the least I can do."

"But, isn't there something else we can do? I mean just walking in there seems risky... the last time you tried to fight this guy, you almost didn't make it out of it alive."

Clayton shook his head. "That's not going to happen this time."

Ruben frowned, growing scared. "Let me help."

"You can't. If you do, the whole pack is sure to attack and then we really don't stand a chance."

"Just... trust me." Clayton placed a hand on Ruben's cheek, pulling him in for a kiss. "He can't beat me this time because I have too much to lose."

"I hope so..." Ruben whispered under his breath.

Clayton glanced at his watch. "We should get going. I don't want to know what happens if we're late."

With no other choice, Ruben nodded and followed his mate further into the forest.

Soon enough, they arrived at the clearing. They looked around but as far as they could tell, the place was deserted. Clayton breathed in deep, trying to pick up on their scent but there was nothing in the air save for the smell of wet leaves and decaying wood.

"What's going on?" Ruben asked, turning in a circle, half expecting the yellow eyes to appear at any moment.

A bird flew overhead, startling them both.

"Something's wrong. Very wrong." Clayton grabbed Ruben by the hand, pulling him close. "I don't like this..."

Suddenly, something fell from the treetops.

Before the men could react, a large net had been thrown over their bodies. Instinctually, they started to struggle which only tangled them up even further.

They fell just as a couple of hulky men jumped down from a couple of nearby trees.

"Fuck," Clayton swore under his breath. He was in the middle of a shift when one of the men jabbed a needle into his arm. He froze as the world became blurry. Blinking didn't help clear away the fog that had rolled into his vision. "What have you done to us?" He asked, clinging to the last tendrils of his strength.

Beside him, Ruben had already collapsed.

"No..." He shook his head. "What have you done to him?" He snarled, losing his temper. He was just about to break free when the drugs took effect and he fell unconscious.

***

A few hours later, Clayton woke up only to find himself tied to a tree trunk. He looked around, spotting Ruben and Beverly nearby, also tied to tree trunks. Their heads were slumped into their chests, skin pale.

It almost looked like they were dead.

No.

They couldn't be dead.

Suddenly, Preston came into view. He laughed, standing there like he had just conquered the entire world. "I always knew you were stupid, but I didn't think you were this stupid. To think that you would walk right into my trap." He shook his head. "Pathetic."

Behind him, a fire blazed, emanating tremendous heat that seemed to burn Clayton's cheeks. He couldn't understand how Preston managed to stand so close to the flame.

Without a word, he grabbed a knife from his belt and thrust it into the fire. The blade turned red as it grew hot. He twisted it this way and that, evening out the heat. When he was satisfied he walked up to

Clayton, a maniacal look on his face. "Now, I'll give you a choice. Either, you can die the easy way. One single blow. Relatively painless. Or, you can choose to save your mate and take the most painful death that I can think of."

"Don't you dare touch him."

Preston shook his head. "You always were emotional. You know, that only leads to weakness."

"I swear to god, if you so much as touch a hair on his head, it'll be the end of you."

"Is that supposed to scare me?" Preston mocked. "We both know that you can't beat me." He snickered. "Just face it, you were never meant to be an alpha. I bet your father is rolling around in his grave right now, horrified by his failure of a son."

"Don't talk about my father!" At that moment, something snapped inside of him. He howled, body tensing and convulsing. The alpha inside of him awoke, coming to its full power.

The transformation was quick – over in the blink of an eye – and suddenly there stood a giant wolf, twice the size of his previous form. Clayton howled at the sun, eyes blazing with hatred.

Without thinking, his body shot into action, dashing forward and throwing Preston into a nearby hut with the swipe of a paw. He crashed right through the wall, splinters penetrating through his skin. He groaned, struggling to get to his feet. Before he could orient himself, Clayton pounced, snarling, exposing his deadly fangs and a second later they sank into Preston's neck. With a flick of his neck, he tore out his throat.

Blood painted his maw, turning his silver fur crimson. His eyes burned with fury.

Once again, he howled. This time, the pack howled back, accepting their newfound leader.

He panted, unable to believe that he had finally defeated his enemy – that Preston – the man that had singlehandedly ruined his life - was dead – that he had killed him.

Eventually, he turned back into his human form and untied Ruben and Beverly who were slowly regaining consciousness.

"What happened?" Ruben mumbled, rubbing his head.

"I finally did what I was supposed to do years ago."

Ruben's eyes widened. "You mean..."

"Yes." Clayton nodded. "He's gone. He won't bother us ever again."

Chapter 17

"So, what now?" Beverly asked, rubbing her wrists. Out of the corner of her eye, she spotted quite a few attractive werewolves and they seemed to be looking at her too.

"Well, technically, I'm supposed to be the alpha."

"What's that mean?" She asked, tilting her head in Clayton's direction, trying to look like someone who was paying attention even though her thoughts were wandering elsewhere.

From a distance, a tan individual with strikingly blonde hair winked at her.

Ruben rolled his eyes. "You can stop drooling now." He said, gently poking her in the side. "Just go talk to him already, will you?"

"Talk to him? Are you crazy? He's a werewolf!"

Ruben pushed her in the direction of the guy she kept ogling at. "I'm a werewolf and you do just fine talking to me." Just then, a couple of female wolves appeared, whisking her away. Soon, they started to giggle amongst themselves, occasionally looking over at the single men.

"Beverly seems to be fitting in just fine," Clayton commented.

"Yeah. I thought for sure she'd freak out once she found out I was a werewolf, but she's handling things quite well. Apparently, she knew about it for a while."

"I see." Clayton started to walk off, veering away from the rest of the pack until they were alone by the fire. A couple of pack members had already disposed of the body. Clayton had taken a bath, washing away all the blood from his fur. In a way, it was like nothing happened. "It must be nice to have such a good friend by your side."

"Yeah, it is," Ruben said with a fond smile.

They sat down together on a nearby log. Clayton took Ruben's hand in his. "I need to ask you something."

Clayton's expression was completely serious and that made Ruben nervous. He gulped, expecting the worst. A million and one scenarios popped up in his head, making him worry.

Silence settled around the couple as Clayton took his time choosing his words. He wet his lips in preparation before taking a deep breath. "Ruben, when we mated, I wasn't really thinking straight. I was so possessed with the need to have you for myself that I didn't even ask you if that's what you wanted."

Ruben looked into his eyes and smiled. "Yes."

"You mean that?"

He nodded. "I was a little unsure at first since, after all, I had never been with a man before and that happened to be my first gay experience. It was amazing, don't get me wrong. But, there was a part of me that struggled to accept that I was really in love with you but now I know, without a doubt, that we were meant for each other. I can feel it in my heart like there are invisible strings bringing us together. Can you feel it too?"

Clayton answered by pulling his mate into a kiss. Their lips collided and exploded into a firework display of emotions. They couldn't contain themselves as their tongues swirled together and their hands roamed along each other's bodies.

Before things could get hot and heavy, however, Clayton pulled away, holding Ruben's face ever so gently in his hands. His thumbs caressed his cheeks as he smiled such a heartwarming smile that it sent butterflies fluttering through Ruben's stomach.

"I love you."

"I love you, too," Ruben whispered, pressing his forehead against his. "So much..."

They remained forehead to forehead for quite a while before Clayton took Ruben's hands and pressed them into his. "I still have one more thing to ask you."

"Okay..."

"These wolves expect me to be their leader – their alpha – and I think I'm finally ready for that responsibility. But, I want you to rule by my side."

Ruben's eyes grew wide. "Me?"

"Who else? You're the one person I trust the most." He paused. "But, I know you are studying to become a nurse and I don't want to get in the way of that. I want you to follow your dreams, whatever they might be."

"Can't I do both?"

"You can. I just didn't want to burden you. But, if you think you can do both then by all means…" Clayton grinned. "And, when you're done with your education, I'm sure the pack could use a nurse on their team. You might even be able to learn a thing or two from our druids."

"Druids?"

"They're untraditional doctors, so to speak. They use herbs from the forest to heal people. Here, let me introduce you." Clayton got up and headed for a hut painted with bright colors in intricately geometric patterns.

Inside, the hut was filled with smoke. Clayton waved it away, revealing an elderly woman with two silver braids that reached all the way down to her woven belt.

"Ruben, I would like you to meet my grandmother, Silvia."

Ruben's eyes widened. "I thought you didn't have a family…"

"My grandmother is the only one left. When the pack rejected me, she was the only one who defended me."

"Of course I did." She interjected with a gravelly voice full of wisdom. "And I would have followed you if it weren't for these old bones!"

Clayton chuckled.

The woman got up and leaning on a cane, she hobbled over, narrowing her eyes in Ruben's direction. She pointed a gnarled finger on the mating mark on the side of his neck. "So, you've finally found the one?"

"I have. What do you think?"

Silvia circled around Ruben's body and sniffed the air before a bright smile painted her face. "I think you got a good one."

"Really?" Ruben said.

"Mhm. You have a good heart. Good aura. You'll do well in your lifetime." She rubbed her chin. "And, you have an interest in medicine?" She asked, raising an eyebrow.

"I'm studying to become a nurse."

"Why don't you become my apprentice instead? Much cheaper and you can start helping people right away."

"Really?"

"Yes. I'll let you think about it."

"Thank you!"

"Of course." She smiled and suddenly wrapped her arms around the young wolf. "Welcome to the family."

And for the first time in his life, Ruben knew what it felt like to belong somewhere.

Chapter 18

After a few days, everything was settled within the pack. Clayton assumed his rightful place as alpha and Ruben was respected as his beta.

Now that Preston was gone, people were free to express themselves and soon the culture flourished. The wolves had a spectacular festival in honor of their new leader complete with dancing and a gigantic bonfire.

"I can't believe it..." Clayton whispered to himself, leaning against a tree and watching the festivities from a distance.

A few seconds later, Ruben returned with two plates filled with food, from smoky BBQ to baked beans. "Maria is one hell of a cook," Ruben commented, nibbling on the chicken leg he had in his hand. "How does she do it?"

Clayton chuckled. "Don't ever ask her for a family recipe. She'll bite your head off."

"Noted." He said as he took another bite of the chicken leg. "But, seriously, this is amazing."

"Wait until you have her world-famous brisket. It's to die for. Trust me."

Ruben licked his lips just thinking about it.

"So, how are you liking things so far?"

"It's great! Everyone's so accepting of us, don't you think?"

Clayton nodded. "If I'm completely honest with you, I'm surprised."

"Why?"

"Because, at one point, most of these people rejected me. They didn't think I would make a suitable leader."

"But, weren't they being influenced by Preston?"

"I guess so."

Just then, Beverly walked up to them. She had a handsome man hanging on her arm. They were both giggling, cheeks red.

"You might want to go easy on the moonshine," Clayton suggested, seeing how drunk they were. "You wouldn't want to get hurt."

"Kevin would never hurt me!" Beverly giggled. "He's one giant teddy bear."

"Teddy wolf."

She hiccupped. "That's right! Teddy wolf!"

"Don't forget, our apprenticeship starts tomorrow morning. Silvia wants us at her hut at the crack of dawn."

"Fuck, really?" Beverly groaned. "Maybe I should switch over to water before I wake up with a hangover."

"But, what's the fun in that?" Keith whispered, nuzzling into her neck.

"Kevin, not in front of the alpha!" She said, feigning modesty as she hit his arm in a playful manner.

Together, they walked away, heading straight to Kevin's hut.

"Looks like they're about to have a happy ending..." Ruben thought aloud.

"Looks like it."

"Do you think she'll be okay living among werewolves?"

"Beverly's a strong girl. I think she'll be just fine." Clayton said, his voice deep and full of wisdom.

"You know, you've changed since becoming the alpha."

"I have?"

"Mhm. You're more serious now. I can tell that you're really trying to take responsibility for the pack."

"I just want it to succeed. I've heard rumors of other packs dying out and I don't want that to happen..." He got up and walked around the fire, throwing in his unwanted bones. They crackled, the bone marrow turning the flames green for a moment before they went back to red.

As he stood there, Ruben couldn't help but notice how impossibly powerful he looked – like a man ready to rule the world. And, it was sexy as hell.

His excitement rose as he thought about all the things they could do together now that they were in a legitimate relationship. He could only imagine how passionate their nights would be, bed rocking, bodies rubbing together, teeth nipping at the skin. Mmm.

Inside his pants, Ruben's member came to life, struggling for freedom. He got up and advanced toward the alpha with one intention in mind. He had to have him.

He slung his arms around his neck and pulled him close, kissing his lips with a fevered passion.

Clayton returned the kiss. He wrapped his arms around Ruben's slender torso until their hips were locked together. "Someone's excited," Clayton whispered, rubbing against his lover's erection. "What has gotten into you?"

"I just couldn't help it, looking at you."

"Oh, is that so?" Clayton asked with a smirk, leaning down so he could kiss the side of his neck. "How badly do you want me?"

"Bad."

"You're going to have to do better than that."

"Come on, don't make me beg. You know just how much I want you... I bet you can smell it on me."

"I can," Clayton answered, smirk deepening. "But I like to see you struggle."

Ruben groaned, letting his hands fall on Clayton's ass, squeezing it between his palms. "You know you want me too. Don't act like this is a one-sided thing. I bet that you're thinking about me and all the things you could do to me. Hell, maybe, you're imagining what it would feel like to bend me over this log and take me right here and now."

"It's tempting." Clayton mused. "But, tonight, I'd rather take you to my bed." And, without another word, he hoisted Ruben into his arms and carried him bridal style into his own personal hut. While most of the other wolves shared communal apartments, the alpha and his beta were allowed their own private home and Clayton was about to make the most of it.

No one said a word as the two of them left the festivities. They knew exactly what was about to happen.

"What are you doing?"

"What does it look like I'm doing?" Clayton asked, an amused look on his face.

"Oh, I don't know..." Ruben answered, acting all innocent.

"You aren't going to be innocent for long, that's for sure," Clayton growled. "Because, tonight, you're all mine and I'm going to do whatever I want with you. The whole pack is going to hear you scream."

Ruben shivered just thinking about it. He grinned and locked eyes with his lover and in that moment, he knew that tonight was going to be one hell of a night.

Chapter 19

As soon as he was close enough, Clayton threw Ruben on the bed.

Before Ruben could respond, Clayton pounced on his lover, pinning his wrists above his head. "Mmm... I like when you do that..." He whispered, arching his back and thrusting his hips into the air, begging for it.

"Do you?" Clayton grinned, nibbling his earlobe. "That's not going to be the only thing you like tonight."

"You're such a tease. How about you stop talking and start doing instead."

"You're so eager." Clayton slipped his hand into Ruben's pants. "Such a naughty boy. I should teach you to be careful what you wish for."

"Maybe you should," Ruben answered, a lustful smirk playing on his lips. "Come on, baby, show me what you're made of."

"Oh, I will, but first, you're going to do me a little favor."

"Oh?" Ruben cocked his head in question.

"On your knees," Clayton demanded.

Ruben shivered, turned on by the authority in his mate's voice. Immediately, he got on his knees, placing his hands on his thighs, mouth open, waiting for it.

Clayton took out his dick, stroking it slowly, getting it nice and hard. "Like what you see?"

"Mhm." Ruben crawled forward, pushing Clayton onto the bed. "I like it very much." Once he was settled between Clayton's legs, he wrapped his lips around his thick girth. He started to move his tongue around the tip, teasing him with it.

Clayton groaned in pleasure, tilting his head back into the pillow. "That feels so good. Don't stop." He tangled his fingers into his hair, pulling on it slightly, forcing him to take his dick further into his mouth until it hit the back of his throat.

Ruben sucked him harder, bobbing his head up and down, faster and faster. His nails dug into Clayton's thighs as he started to deep throat his mate, doing everything he could to make him feel good. While he did so, his hands played with his balls, fondling and squeezing them.

Soon, it was too much for Clayton to handle. He pushed Ruben off his cock and threw him back. A second later, he pulled him into his lap, pinned him against the wall, and kissed him hard.

The kiss left him breathless. Ruben melted into it, wrapping his arms around his neck, tugging on his hair as they grinded into one another. At this point, Ruben was so horny that he felt like he would go insane if he didn't orgasm soon. His hormones raged, and his inner wolf howled. "Quit playing around, let's do this..."

"Patience." Clayton nipped his mating mark, sending a wave of pleasure running through Ruben's body.

He moaned out.

The sound made Clayton growl with desire. He pushed Ruben against the wall once more, kissing him harder than ever. This time, he pulled out Ruben's cock and started to stroke it nice and hard, pushing him toward the brink of climax.

"Clayton!" Ruben screamed, arching his back. "I'm going to cum."

"Not yet." Clayton threw him onto the bed, pushing his head onto the mattress and pulling his ass into the air. "That's better." Suddenly, he plunged into the tight hole.

Ruben cried out, struggling to accommodate Clayton's massive cock. His toes curled with pleasure and his balls tightened as his pleasure washed over every inch of his body. "Mmm. That feels so good."

"You haven't seen anything yet," Clayton promised, slowly pulling out only to ram back in again. He kept this up for a while, bring them both to an orgasmic high but never quite pushing them over the edge.

"Please..." Ruben begged.

Clayton pulled on his hair, exposing his neck. His tongue darted forward, flicking over the mark, sending spasm after spasm of ecstasy coursing through his veins.

"That's it, scream for me!"

"Fuck!" Ruben moaned louder and louder as every inch of Clayton's cock penetrated him, making him feel like he was about to burst with the size of it. At the same time, he loved every second of it.

Suddenly, Clayton started to fuck him so hard that the bed began to rock, creaking under their movements.

"We're going to break the bed..." Ruben gasped, clutching at the sheets, trying to ground himself in the moment. "Fuck... it feels so good, don't stop."

Clayton pulled his hair even harder, fucking him like an animal.

"Please..."

"Not yet," Clayton growled, slapping his lover's ass, leaving behind a red handprint. A second later, his cock started to throb inside his hole. "You're so tight..."

The bed continued to rock, the bedposts swaying.

And then, they cracked altogether and then collapsed onto the ground.

The two lovers fell into a fit of laughter.

"I love you."

"I love you too." Ruben smiled, kissing his mate ever so gently. "No one has ever made me feel this happy before."

"I'm glad. Now, let's keep it that way." Slowly, Clayton started to rock his hips.

Soon, they both started to moan in pleasure, bodies shaking.

"I'm going to cum."

"Cum for me, baby."

Almost on demand, Ruben exploded, shooting string after string of sticky cum onto the bed sheets.

A second later, Clayton pulled out and decorated his lover's ass with his seed.

Together, they fell onto the bed, tangled in each other's embrace. Ruben rested his head on Clayton's chest, listening to the steady rhythm of his heart. It comforted him, making him feel safe. It seemed, so long as they were together, that nothing could ever go wrong.

Clayton tightened his embrace and wrapped his legs around Ruben's torso, cocooning him against his body. "Nothing is ever going to take you away from me." He whispered, kissing the top of his head.

"Good, because I never want to leave your side."

"Do you really mean that?"

Ruben nodded. "As far as I'm concerned, I want to grow old with you. To start a family with you."

Clayton smiled, knowing, one day, those things would come true.

Epilogue

Three years later.

"Make sure you crush the iris before you leave," Silvia said as she stared into the fire.

"I've already crushed the iris. I've placed the paste in a jar just as you asked."

"What about the Marigold? Have you put it out to dry?"

"Yes."

The old woman nodded, reading her hands on the top of her walking stick. "You've been an excellent pupil these past three years. I think it's about time you take my place as the healer of the pack."

"Oh no, I have a lot more to learn."

"But I am getting old."

Ruben shook his head. "You're still young at heart!"

"But not young in body. This body is failing me more and more every day. It becomes difficult to walk – difficult to live. Soon, it will be my time to go."

"Don't say such things. You still have many more years ahead of you."

"I would not be so sure." She turned her head, laying her cataract-ridden eyes on the young man turned druid. "All things come to an end. It is not a point of remorse and sadness. I will be reunited with my ancestors. I will once again see my husband."

"You've told me much about him."

"He was a kind man. Clayton used to love his grandfather. You know, he was the one who taught Clayton how to hunt."

Ruben smiled, imagining what the alpha wolf looked like as a child.

"But as I've said, my time has come. You and Beverly will take over my profession."

"Beverly is about to get married, you know."

"I do."

"She'll be busy."

"She'll show up when you need her most. Trust me." Silvia answered with a knowing smile. "She always does."

Ruben couldn't argue with that. Even though his best friend had started her life with Kevin, they were nonetheless inseparable. They told each other everything and even worked together, helping injured pack members from the elderly to the pups.

"Is there anything else you'd like me to do?" Ruben asked, placing a hand on the woman's shoulder.

"No. Go on and enjoy the rest of your day."

"Alright," Ruben said with a smile, leaving the healing hut and heading home.

Overhead, the sun was just starting to set. The sky was painted in a faded purple that stretched across the horizon. The forest shimmered, leaves dancing in the wind.

Ruben took his time, enjoying the walk.

When he got home, he expected to find Clayton in his office, working on a new treaty with a neighboring pack but to his surprise, the house seemed empty. "Babe? Are you home?" He called out but there was no response. "Babe?"

Silence.

"Strange... where could he be?" Ruben thought aloud as he searched through all the rooms. They were all empty. "Huh."

Eventually, he stepped into the backyard.

To his surprise, it was decorated in a tropical theme.

"Hello," Clayton whispered, coming up behind him and pulling him into a hug. He kissed his neck, gently leaving behind a trail of kisses. "How was your day?" He asked, ignoring the fact that there were fake palm trees in the backyard. Or that there was a kiddie pool complete with a pink flamingo floatie.

"Good..." Ruben answered hesitantly. "But... what is all this...?"

"Well, as I'm sure you know, it's our anniversary."

"Yes..."

"And, I've been promising to take you on vacation for a while now, but something always gets in the way. I was going to take you out this time around but then the treaty got in the way. I figured this would be the next best option."

Ruben smiled. "You did all of this for me?"

"Of course." Clayton pulled them into a nearby lawn chair, letting Ruben sit in his lap. "I wanted to make it special."

"This is amazing."

"You really think so?"

"I do." Ruben leaned back, resting his head on Clayton's shoulder. "You always manage to make me smile."

"I'm glad. That's all I want to do. Keep you happy."

They held hands and looked up at the sky for a while. Ruben couldn't help but think that life was perfect. He finally had the life that he always wanted.

"You know, Beverly's going to get married."

"I heard." Clayton nodded.

"She has really assimilated into the pack. It's almost like she's one of us."

"She might become a werewolf soon enough."

Ruben widened his eyes in surprise. "What do you mean?"

"If Kevin decides to mate with her – to mark her – then she will transform into a werewolf."

"Really?"

"Mhm. It allows a female to carry the pups without getting hurt. It's one of the reasons why werewolves have been able to survive for so long."

"I see... there's still so much for me to learn."

"One day at a time." Clayton mused, his voice full of wisdom. He had matured incredibly during his three years as alpha. He now saw the world in a new light.

Time passed.

Soon, it was dark.

The flame of the nearby fire danced on their faces. Ruben was close to falling asleep when Clayton roused him. "There's something I have to ask you."

"What?"

Clayton got up and reached into his pocket.

Before Ruben knew what was going on, Clayton got down on one knee and looked up at his lover. "These past three years have been nothing but wonderful. I know we already mated but I want us to be more than that. So..." He paused, opening the tiny jewelry box, revealing a beautiful ring made of silver and etched with the Celtic knot around its circumference. "... will you marry me?"

Ruben stared in a state of disbelief.

Was this really happening?

He gulped, heart beating fast. His palms grew sweaty.

For a minute, he didn't know what to do, brain blank.

Suddenly, he smiled wide and lunged forward. "Yes, a thousand times yes." And with a passionate kiss, they sealed their fate together.

*****

Don't miss out!

Visit the website below and you can sign up to receive emails whenever Van Cole publishes a new book. There's no charge and no obligation.

https://books2read.com/r/B-A-RTRV-ZKVCC

BOOKS 2 READ

Connecting independent readers to independent writers.

Also by Van Cole

3 Man Huddle: MMM Best Friend Romance
His Alpha Wolf: Gay First Time Romance
A Dragon's Miracle: Gay Dragon MPREG Romance
Double-Teamed: MMM First Time Football Romance
His Football Star: Gay Second Chance Romance
Love In My Town: MM First Time Romance
Training A Hockey Star
Game Night
Double Shift
Take A Shot
Dear Professor
Getting Inked
Ninth Inning
Triple Threat
Seducing My Best Friend's Brother
My Protector
The Blueprint
Show Me The Way
End Zone
Matched To His Tiger
Love At First Puck
My Straight Boss
Falling For The Alpha
My Boss
On Thin Ice

www.ingramcontent.com/pod-product-compliance
Lightning Source LLC
Chambersburg PA
CBHW021958170726
47994CB00021B/980